I S.P.I.
Surf & Turf

෨෴

Michelle Lee

Blue Forge Press
Port Orchard ✿ Washington

I S.P.I.: Surf and Turf
Copyright April 2021
by Michelle Lee

Blue Flash #0005

First Print Edition April 2021

Blue Forge Press is the print division of the volunteer-run, federal 501(c)3 nonprofit company, Blue Legacy, founded in 1989. Dedicated to empowering artisans marginalized due to race, age, ability, sexuality or economics, we have four divisions: Blue Forge Press, Blue Forge Films, Blue Forge Gaming, and Blue Forge Records. Find out more about us at www.MyBlueLegacy.org and www.BlueForgePress.com

Blue Forge Press
7419 Ebbert Drive Southeast
Port Orchard, Washington 98367
blueforgepress@gmail.com
360-550-2071 ph.txt

In loving memory of
Risa, Dan, Gage, and Jameson

I S.P.I.

Surf & Turf

❦

Michelle Lee

Chapter One

I kicked my feet back onto my desk and the ancient office chair supporting my finely rounded buttocks gave a wail like rusty fornicating ducks that were swimming in boiling water. The back of my head bounced on the floor where I was deposited and the chair shot out from under me as if it were a greased sled on compacted snow.

The resulting sound of old metal meeting a crumbling office wall blended with the curse words that spewed from my mouth in a bout of verbal diarrhea. Perfect. Hopefully, no other tenants in the high-class building saw my fall from grace. The thought of this place being high-class made me snort but it's where my business, I S.P.I., was housed. Supernatural Paranormal Investigator.

Risa Daniels is my name. I'm a spy, or at least that's what I liked to say. A P.I., or S.

P.I., a bounty hunter, a mother, along with a list of other titles bestowed on me by many who thought less favorably of me. Some not so savory. I couldn't begin to tell you what race I was; my gene pool is heavily chlorinated. My parents were the equivalent of magical hippies.

There were no racial lines in my history. I stem from a long line of free love, break the race chains, sleep with everyone, and be a little of everything; only the magical waters become muddy and powers become diluted. Thanks, mom and dad, for that kick in the girl nards.

I know that I have some fairy blood in me but I didn't get any of their cool elemental magic. Let me rephrase that. I have some of it but it doesn't work when I want it to, only when it's the worst timing possible. I got the fairy longevity, though. There's a trace of pixie blood in the mix and I did get tiny wings, but I can't fly and much like the fairy magic, they appear at inopportune moments. There has to be siren

D.N.A. somewhere down the line, but it only seems to work when I'm on the phone and people mistake me for being the type to deliver a telephonic happy ending. I am positive that there is a good percentage of leprechaun because I get lucky a lot, not just between the sheets. You probably get the picture by now; I'm a magical mutt.

I have three sons and it shouldn't come as any shock to you that there are, of course, three different baby daddies. I have no defense to that other than I was young. Remember the longevity thing? I'm about three hundred and seventy-two years old, as a rough estimate. What? I'm still a woman; I can't reveal my actual age.

My oldest son, Gavin, was an oops, surprise, you're going to be a teenage mother type of pregnancy. His father was a troll. Literal and figurative. Stupid teenage hormones and tequila. I have to say, screwing a troll as your first lover at eighteen, not the best choice. Size matters and that hurt. Anyway, Gavin tends to take after his father a bit with the attitude, which isn't all that pleasant. He's my son, and I still love him, even when I want to wrap my hands around his neck and squeeze.

My middle son, Gage, is about the sweetest boy ever to have lived. I'm not biased; everyone that knows him says that. He was named Gage because my meter of picking good men was broken like the gauge needed replacing. I'm awful, I know. Gage's father was a selkie. Someone captured him and skinned him when Gage was five. Glad he was useful to someone during his life.

Then there is my youngest, Jameson. If you are wondering about his name, that was what I had been drinking the night I met his father. I had to switch it up since the tequila didn't produce good results. Come to think of it; I shouldn't drink. I digress; Jameson is a joy. Equal parts devil and angel, which makes sense since his dad is a fallen angel. I should have figured that would mean he wouldn't be faithful. Oh well.

I live in Glimmering Rock, a magical

city hidden within a large human bustling town called Branstone. Here is where it all gets complicated. Humans, supernatural beings, magical beings, paranormal beings, myths, and legends, all live in harmony. Of course, that is because humans have no idea we exist and live among them.

Glimmering Rock had a magical council where the heads of the prominent races made laws. By that, I mean the ones that have the most population within the city. Then there was the law enforcement for us magical types, separate from the council, and then human law enforcement, and finally, the black market in both worlds often intertwined amongst all of them. Then there was me.

All of the groups knew who I was. Some respected me; others thought of me as a joke. A scant few were terrified of me, those were the smart ones, and the rest only thought of me when they needed someone not affiliated with any of the authorities. I worked in a substantial gray area.

The cases I took on depended on the client that walked through my barely still hanging office door. Human or magical, I worked for both. Beggars can't be choosers and living isn't free. A girl's gotta do what a girl's gotta do to make the mortgage payment.

It was the moment that I was bent over; my ass pointed right at the door to my office while wiping my hands on my shins and trying not to pee myself when I sneezed from the dust that kicked up that a would-be client walked in. My luck didn't work in this instance.

At the sound of a clearing throat, I righted myself as quickly as possible, squeezed my legs together as if that would hold in the pee, and pivoted on my heels. My blond hair fanned out around my face, the ends whipping me in the eyeball before it settled back down. With my green eyes watering like a mud puddle after being stomped in by a rambunctious three-year-old, I smiled.

"Hello," I managed to get out while the potential client picked up my chair and slid it back across the room to me.

"Ms. Daniels, I presume?" the man said with one of those deep, rumbly, gravel caught in his throat voices.

Thank goodness I wasn't drinking; I'd have tried to put moves on him. "Correct. Thank you for your assistance. My chair was tired of me and hit the eject button."

"No complaints," the man who would be my latest mistake smiled. He had dimples. "The view was pleasurable."

I was doomed. I caught myself before readjusting my boobs, which had managed to work their way free during my meeting with the floor. I didn't need to call attention to them; his eyes kept wandering that direction of their own volition.

"How can I help you?" I sat down, putting my elbows on my desk in front of me, trying to block the lumpy boobs from sight. I made it a point not to sleep with people who hired me. Was it wrong to hope he didn't hire me?

"Let me make my entrance again," the man smiled and stepped back into the hallway, closing the door behind him.

Not one to look a gift horse in the mouth, I quickly set my boobs back where they belonged, smoothed my shirt down, and tried to strike a feminine pose and look classy. Total long shot but I had to try for my pride's sake.

The rickety door opened and the good-looking man stepped back inside with a brilliant smile, his eyes dropping to my chest. Biting back laughter was brutal and how I managed was beyond me. He took a seat across from me and held out his hand.

"Ms. Daniels, correct? My name is Ivan and I'm looking to hire an investigator," he introduced himself as I shook his hand. "May I ask what the initials in your business name mean?"

Rough skin, calloused palms, dirt under his nails, firm grip, and large knuckles, I cataloged quickly. Ivan was a man who was used to manual labor, outdoor work if I had to guess. Non-magical, as that familiar zap of energy failed to materialize when our skin touched.

"Call me Risa," I answered, releasing his hand after the quick thought of wondering what it would feel like undressing me passed. "Sexy private investigator. What can I do for you?"

"You have an interesting reputation, Risa," Ivan started with a giant grin. He leaned back into the plastic chair, and when it creaked, I desperately hoped it didn't break under him. Ivan crossed an ankle over his knee and grinned at me again. "I have an open case with the police department in Branstone. However, I'm not sure they can help me."

The barking laugh that came out of my mouth surprised us both. I coughed, not in the least embarrassed. "Why do you think that?"

The police of Branstone were an eclectic bunch. They had a few good cops in the department and those cops knew of both cities. There were also clueless cops that wouldn't know a unicorn from a rhinoceros.

"Because when I told them that my cows were disappearing, they asked me if they were in my freezer," Ivan replied with a straight face. "I'd probably know if I butchered one of my cows. The cop took my statement and opened a case, yet I am almost certain they won't investigate it."

Hmm, that response didn't tell me if Ivan knew of Glimmering Rock and its inhabitants or not. All it told me was he didn't have faith in the officers charged with protecting his life. Not a stretch to agree with him.

"Branstone does have a few inepts on the squad," I agreed. "Do you think someone is stealing your cows? Or is your suspicion something more insidious?"

I was happy to note my assessment was right on the dot about him working outdoors. If Ivan had cows, he was a rancher or farmer. A hand reveals a lot about a person; I was also very observant. Ivan was correct that I had a reputation.

I was a thorn in the sides of all the authorities, not because I walked a thin line between lawful and blatantly illegal, but because I got answers when they couldn't. I might be a bit unorthodox but I closed all my cases.

"I'm not entirely sure." Ivan sighed and ran a hand through his hair. I am sure he had no idea that it was sexy, and if he did, who cares? "I noticed the first one missing about a month ago. I marked it in my log and noted where her last position was. I chalked it up to a natural predator. I'm aware these things happen on full moons."

Ah, he did know of us then. I pulled out a pad of paper and started taking notes. "Okay, so it happened on the full moon?"

"That was the first one I noticed, yes." Ivan let out a frustrated breath. "I had a deal with the pack alpha to notify me if one of his pack got a little carried away. He promised to make restitution but when I questioned him he firmly told me I was wrong in my assumption that one of his killed a cow."

Talk with Mick, I noted. "Firmly told you? Did he get aggressive with you?"

"I wouldn't call it aggressive; Mick was irritated with me for not believing him," Ivan corrected. "He's never lied to me before so I accepted his explanation and went back home. I poured over the security feeds for hours and saw not one wolf on my land. That was when I started to pay closer attention. About a week after the full moon, another cow went missing."

I wrote down the date and another tally for the cow. "Only one?"

"Yes. It was two cows total at that point. Three days later, four cows went missing. This time, I saw a blip on the camera. It was almost as if the camera had skipped itself. It was that quick. I took the footage to a friend of mine who is a tech person and he could see nothing that would indicate equipment failure or someone messing with the feed. Six cows disappearing creates a lot of missing income in my line of work. My ranch has both dairy and beef cattle and it was exactly three of each," Ivan supplied, his tone growing agitated. "All females."

"I understand. What is your friend's name?" I asked, noting it all. If I were Ivan, I would have suspected the pack as well. "Also, did you take this to the Glimmering Rock police?"

"Danny Reese," Ivan filled in the blank. "No, he suggested I speak to you and bypass the police."

Startled a bit at the admission, I tried to keep my face blank. I was sure I looked constipated. "Okay," I drew out the word.

Ivan laughed. "He said you were unconventional, but there was no one better. He also warned me you don't sleep with clients."

"There are a lot of things I'd do for a paycheck, but sex isn't one of them," I blurted out automatically. Of all the people, Ivan's friend was a booty call of mine. "Nice of him to share that."

Ivan's warm laugh made me want to abandon that rule. I kept taking notes as Ivan shared his ordeal. We discussed my fees, had a frank conversation about sex that made me pick up the phone and call Danny as soon as Ivan left to arrange a hook-up. It was probably the bastard's plan from the start.

Chapter Two

I had to admit that I wasn't expecting a case of missing cows to land in my lap. Humans stealing cows wasn't unheard of and happened more than people thought. However, in a magical city hidden within the human one, it wasn't a common occurrence.

The police should take anything affecting someone's livelihood seriously and my first stop was going to be the underground market. If someone was selling off stolen cows, chances are someone there would know about it. The trick would be getting those people to open up.

Reliable magic would be handy in this situation. With my mixed bloodlines, that wouldn't be happening anytime soon. Disaster would strike first. Thankfully, my leprechaun genes work in my favor most of the time. Plus, my dad made sure I knew how to fight physically since my magic couldn't dependably defend me when things went south, as they often did in the market.

I might also run into Gavin down there. He occasionally sold some of his goods there and, like a good mother, I didn't ask where he obtained them so I could plead ignorance if he got caught. I didn't condone his actions, don't get me wrong, but I wasn't above using him as a source either since he was shady anyway.

I slammed my old 1967 CJ5 door and winced at the way the old Jeep shuddered. She needed some tender loving care. For that to happen, I needed a payday. I patted the faded red paint and cooed some unintelligible words at her before I walked away.

The underground market wasn't underground, at least not entirely. It was a hidden pocket inside the magically enhanced parking garage. If a non-magical human drove in here and parked, they wouldn't think anything of the structure. A magical person would see a mirror image of the spaces whichever way they looked.

It was powerful fairy magic with layered illusions over glamour spells. No matter how many times you come here, it always appears the same and it's disorienting. The parking garage itself was linked to a popular shopping mall in Branstone and typically overflowing with the non-magical variety of humans. Yet, the garage always looked practically empty due to some nefarious fairy's intricate spell that wanted the market to remain extremely difficult to find.

For those individuals who made frequent trips to the market, one drain in the garage floor was the starting point on how to find the doorway, and it never looked the same. Fairies were deceptive creatures without breaking the not able to lie trait. Man, do I ever wish that my fairy magic worked.

The concrete jungle I was in was always cooler than the temperature outside the structure; dim and oddly silent. To make it even harder, you were dodging cars that appeared out of nowhere as they exited the garage. Getting out was far more straightforward than you'd think with all this magic.

Locating the drain, I counted fifteen steps to the east, turned clockwise, and moved another twenty steps. Inhaling slowly, I closed my eyes. This last part was always some mental challenge. Today it looked like you were going to step off the edge of a floor to plummet to your death.

Reflexively, I put my hands out in front of me as I stepped into the abyss and entered the market. My luck held and I didn't smack into anyone and quickly moved to the side in case anyone was coming in behind me.

This little pocket dimension of the market looked like an outdoor bazaar. Booths and tents lined the floors with every type of vendor you could imagine. Looking for a spell to make your farts smell better? The market had it. Not that I ever went and sought that out. It was just an example, I swear.

There was never a set location for any given booth or tent. It changed daily and someone led me to believe that sites were on a first-come, first-serve basis. I tended to think that the vendors that greased the palms enough got to pick wherever they wanted. You'd think it would be in the same place so that it was easier to find them; only that was the reason it was never in the same location.

Conveniently, there was always a spell booth near the entrance that sold locator spells to help you find what you wanted if you were in a hurry. I was and I wasn't. My motherly instincts told me Gavin was here and I simply followed them.

I went down a level and caught the scent of brimstone and vanilla cupcakes. Damn it, what was Jameson doing here? I quickened my step, rounded a corner, and almost walked right into Gavin's father. How could I have not smelled him?

"Risa," Braxton growled. "What brings you here?"

"I'd ask you the same thing, but I don't give a shit. Where's Gavin?" I tried to push my way around the troll. He was immovable.

"He's busy. What do you want?" Braxton stepped closer to me. "I don't need you harassing my son."

"*Your* son?" I screeched, drawing attention. "Why is it now that he's doing shit in the market that he's your son? Yet when I was raising him alone, you demanded a test to prove he was yours and still didn't support him!"

"Shut up, woman!" Braxton snarled the words at me and boxed me in against a wall. "You don't need to spread lies at the top of your lungs. You were fast enough to fuck me senseless and stupid enough not to take precautions."

All these years later and the dumbass troll still made me see red. "Ass-clown. Move!" I demanded with a swift knee to his nuts. Who's the stupid one that left them unprotected?

"Idiot! Mom, are you okay?" Gavin asked, yanking me away from getting head-butted as Braxton doubled over.

"Fine. We need to talk," I told Gavin. I executed a lovely donkey kick behind me into Braxton's ass, shoving him right over to the head-down ass-up position he liked to demand females get in.

Gavin led me to a small booth with some questionable potions displayed on a decorative silk scarf. Nice to see he was trying to make his wares look pretty. I refrained from rolling my eyes and followed him behind a curtain, where I found Jameson sitting and reading a potion book.

"Explain," I demanded of the two.

"You said you wanted to talk?" Gavin tried to steer the conversation away from the reason my youngest son (though, can two hundred and two be considered young?) was reading a book on potion-making.

"Asking for an explanation is talking,"

I pointed out heatedly. "Jameson?"

"It's only research, Mom," Jameson answered without looking up.

"Yeah, research," Gavin echoed, a guilty look crossing his face. "What's up?"

I'd pry the answers out of Jameson later. "What do you know about cows?"

"They make delicious cheeseburgers and milk," Gavin responded with a grin. "Odd question to come find me at the market to ask."

I fought the impulse to laugh and strangle him at the same time. "Not what I meant, smart ass. Has there been talk down here about cows? Cows are going missing in town."

Something flickered across Gavin's face and was gone the next instant. "Not that I've heard. Are they being killed?"

I searched his face for a clue that would tell me he was lying. "I can't say for sure. They are just gone without a trace."

"It's not like you can stuff one in your pocket and get away," Jameson looked up from his book. "There has to be some sign as to what is happening. You sure get interesting cases, Mom."

Gavin frowned at his brother. "I'll keep an ear out for any talk or information. That's an odd enough thing I can't ask around about without raising suspicion," he told me as he looked back at me.

"I'd appreciate it. What's your sperm donor want?" I changed the subject.

There was that look on Gavin's face again. Whatever Braxton wanted wasn't good and he was dragging Gavin into it with him. I should have kicked him twice for good measure. Even at eighteen, when I decided to test out my sexual prowess with him, he was a waste of oxygen.

"Dad asked me to procure some special items for him," Gavin answered cagily. "Client confidentiality and all that. You know how it goes."

"Right." I scowled at my son. "Client confidentiality," I echoed sarcastically. "Don't wind up in jail for the man who wouldn't even acknowledge that he was your father until he was forced to by the court."

"Oh, that reminds me," Jameson stood up. "Dad asked if you were dating anyone."

I winced and started to back away. "Please tell me you didn't say I was single."

"No, I don't think dating him again would do either of you any good," Jameson said with a smile. "He's just looking to get laid anyway."

It was time for me to escape. Danny was waiting for me and he'd take care of my getting laid issue without any entanglements or child production. The most uncomplicated ex to deal with was the one that got skinned and that was because he was dead. May he rest in mostly peace.

"Okay, I'm going to leave now." I pointed to the book Jameson still held and caught his eye. "We'll be talking."

"I love you, Mom." Jameson moved to hug me. "Be safe."

"Love you." Gavin gave me a half-hug. "I'll listen."

It was the best I could ask for under the circumstances. I left and took the circuitous route out, window shopping, or giving the appearance that I was. I didn't have extra money to spend on black market trinkets that may or may not work as advertised. The exercise's point was to surreptitiously listen to those tents where I knew the lips were loose.

I picked up on chatter about a new player that had moved into town. Apparently, he liked to throw money around and had a party boy vibe to him. I made a mental note to find out who he was and avoid him before he became another wrong choice.

I was almost to the exit when I felt that telltale prickle of magic inside me reacting to something. It typically happened when I was in imminent danger and wasn't aware of it. I immediately suspected my baby daddy with the bruised balls and slowed my step. Trolls weren't the brightest of creatures.

I grabbed hold of the building magic inside me and fervently hoped that it worked as I wanted it to perform. Stepping closer to the wall on my left, I turned in the direction I thought the danger was approaching from and prepared to let loose with whatever I could, only nothing was there.

When a hand touched my shoulder from the other side, I spun and released my hold on the magic. You'd think with as many years as I've dealt with faulty magic, I would know better to trust that it would be beneficial to me.

Elemental magic burst from my body in the form of ice. The ground around me turned to a sheet of it and my feet lost their purchase on the floor. Fortunately, I also wiped out whoever had touched me and caused the magical misfire.

In a tangle of limbs and one soon to be bruised ass, I went down hard. Unfortunately, the perpetrator landed directly across my midsection, whooshing the air from my body and winding up with a face in my crotch as the mystery man tried righting himself.

He took his sweet time getting up after that, too. With warm palms planted on my thighs, the man righted himself carefully, trying not to slip on the icy ground. I could feel the stares of the market's patrons at the spectacle I'd made and I wanted up, now.

I shoved the man and used the force to push myself out of his way and took note of the convoluted magic smell. It gave me my first look at him. Damn, he was hot enough to make my underwear melt. If my stomach didn't feel like a unicorn had gored me, I would have appreciated the face in my crotch moment more.

"I'm so sorry," the man said in the most unexpected voice I could have imagined. It was high-pitched, fingernails being peeled back by a toothpick with acid on it type sound. "I shouldn't have startled you."

"You think?" I guffawed, thankful that some retort didn't pop out about his voice.

"The ice magic would have been more effective if you had aimed it about twelve inches in front of you," the man said in a helpful tone.

"I repeat, you think?" I snapped and clawed my way up the wall to standing. "Do you mind getting the hell out of my way now so I can leave?"

"Sure. I'm new to town and wanted to ask you where is the best place to get invisibility potions? My name is Wiley, by the way," the ridiculously handsome man held his hand out to me.

It was the guy the people had been talking about and he was looking for invisibility potions; an interesting fact I filed away for further examination. "You're in the right place. Excuse me."

"Uh, sure." Wiley frowned and moved.

I slipped past him and kept going

without introducing myself. He was trouble. I found it curious that cows go missing and the new man in town was looking for invisibility potions. Way too coincidental, but still noteworthy for picking apart when I wasn't running away from an embarrassing situation that I caused.

Chapter Three

The sizzle of the magic brushed across my skin as I exited back into the parking garage while I rubbed my sore backside. I glanced at my watch before heading to my Jeep. I still had time to burn before I was supposed to meet up with Danny and I didn't want to be early. I'd look desperate.

I decided to stop off at the police station and check-in with the officer assigned to Ivan's case. It wasn't necessary on my part but I liked to extend the courtesy that they usually didn't if our cases crossed paths. The last time it happened, I got accused of interfering with an ongoing investigation.

I knew it wasn't likely that they were actively investigating the cow disappearances but they should be. Vanishing livestock didn't happen every day. Poor Ivan. I didn't know his bank account balance and all I had to base my judgment on was his lack of arguing with my fees. And the fact that he had an active and working ranch, I had to assume that he had funds, yet commiserated with the lack of evidence in the disappearing investment that made him those funds.

I stopped dead in my tracks as my Jeep came into sight. All four tires were flat; the Jeep was resting on the rims. Fury tore through me so fast I didn't have time to try and quell the magic and it appeared in the form of a mini-tornado that ripped through the parking garage.

I dropped and kissed the pavement before the violent wind could flatten me into the position I assumed. Feeling my clothes wanting to be forcefully removed by the product of my instant rage, I could do nothing but wait and hope that I remained clothed when it died out. My saving grace was no one else was in the vicinity that I had to worry about protecting.

Luckily, with my wonky magic, the tornado lost steam relatively quickly. "Could have at least refilled my tires with that air, you useless magic," I muttered as I wiped my hands on my pants.

Grateful that the clients I'd recently helped had all paid in full, so there was money in my account, I fished my phone from my pocket and called my insurance company to come to fix my tires. Whoever had done it hadn't slashed them at least. They'd only let all the air out.

I leaned against my Jeep while I waited and called Gage, hoping that he might know what his brothers were up to regarding potions. Jameson and Gage were relatively close-knit. Gavin was usually the one who kept his distance from the other two.

Gage's phone rang and went to voicemail. "Gage, it's Mom. Call me when you have a moment," I spoke after the annoying beep. "I need info."

Hanging up, I looked around the seemingly empty parking garage. I knew there were other cars here. I could hear the sounds of people closing doors, engines starting, tires squealing, but thanks to the magic, I couldn't see them. Disconcerting when I was stuck waiting for assistance in a magical parking garage that they might not be able to see me in.

Not sure why that thought hadn't clicked when I made the phone call, I slammed the palm of my hand against my forehead. Idiot. In all these years, this wasn't a situation I had dealt with before. Even still, it's not like I didn't know it was a place imbued with more spells than a witch's grimoire.

With a heavy sigh, I lifted myself to standing upright and wondered if I'd be able to push the Jeep outside the entrance to the garage. Thanks to my muddy bloodlines, I was stronger than a typical person. It wouldn't hurt to try, I guess.

I walked around to the driver's side and opened the door. Climbing in, I shifted it into neutral, got out slowly, positioned my body so the door didn't slam into my back too hard, and began to push. It's an old Jeep, I've had to move it this way before but that was with air in the tires.

I managed to move the Jeep about a foot with some serious effort. Another couple of feet and I was drenched with sweat and thankful that I didn't drive a large, heavy vehicle. I wasn't sure how long the attempt had taken me but I was about ready to kiss the driver of the roadside assistance truck when he appeared from nowhere.

"Miss Sanders?" the man who was my new hero asked.

"Yes! Thank you!" I cried. I stopped myself from throwing my arms around his neck and managed only to smile. "I don't think there are any holes, but it looks like someone let all the air out of my tires. I was trying to push the Jeep out to the street where it would be easier for you to find me."

"I'll take a look," he smiled back, and I saw the name on his shirt said Tim.

I made another mental note to call the insurance company and sing the man's praises. I stepped to the side as he got busy and, after a few minutes, he determined the same thing I did. Someone had only let out the air; no one punctured anything. He pulled out an air compressor and got to work refilling the tires with air.

"You'll probably need to replace the tires soon. The tread is getting low," Tim told me helpfully.

"It's on my list of things to do," I replied, already knowing that bit of information.

"Gotta love these old Jeeps. They run forever and are almost indestructible," Tim kept up the friendly banter with me. "Collector items, as well, if I'm not mistaken."

I wanted to laugh. It was brand new when I bought it. Tim wasn't wrong, though; these old Jeeps were fantastic. "She's my old girl and I'll love her forever."

He finished up with the tires, shook my hand, gave me a flirty smile, and took off. I rechecked the time and realized I needed to head to Danny's house. There wasn't time for me to check in at the police station now. I would have to either do it tomorrow or later this afternoon.

I jumped into the Jeep with fatigued muscles and made my way to my current booty call's residence. Danny, being a tech guy and all, made good money. Me, not making good money and being a stubborn female, refused his help along with his offer of a more committed relationship. I'd more than proved I wasn't good at relationships at this point in my life and saw no need to torture him by tying him to me.

Poor guy didn't deserve that outcome. Besides, I liked the arrangement we had. Some days I needed my alone time and solitude after a day of playing with the scourge of humanity. That seemed to be what most of the cases were dealing with when the client walked through my door.

What Danny and I had was fun, mutually satisfactory in the sex department, and it might be wrong, but I was happy that I could walk away if I needed to. Not that I wanted to do that, it was just a peace of mind that it gave me knowing I could. My three baby daddies were mistakes but they each gave me something I treasured.

By the time I pulled into Danny's driveway, I was horny beyond belief and dismayed to find three other vehicles present. With a sigh, I dropped to my feet, rubbed my tailbone, and trudged up the porch and let myself in. I followed the sound of voices back to Danny's office.

The sight that greeted me was one of three locals talking to Danny about hacking someone's computer or equally ridiculous shit that I didn't want to hear. I wasn't precisely law enforcement, and I skirted the law several times throughout the day. However, I didn't blatantly break it.

One of the men, Petey, looked over towards me as I leaned in the doorway. "Lookin' for a good time, sugar?"

"You wouldn't know how to give a woman a good time, Petey," I replied with a smirk. "Not even if she drew you a detailed cartoon map using the easy words and bright arrows pointing to the right areas."

"Danny is a computer nerd; you think he knows?" Petey fired back.

"He didn't need a map, which is a good indication. Also, I keep coming back for more. What does that tell you?" I cocked my hip out and bit back a laugh as Petey looked me over.

The second man, whose name evades me, barked out a harsh laugh. "Poor Petey got shut down by a woman for the millionth time today."

"If you gentlemen are done, I think this conversation is over," Danny said as he stood. "I can't help you this time."

"You can; you just won't," Petey turned from me and glared at Danny. "You just want to get laid now that your flavor of the month is here."

"I think you are done with your tongue wagging, Petey," I interjected. "Time for you to go so Danny can get to wagging his tongue and tasting the flavor of the month, which happens to be a favorite of his."

I pushed off the doorframe, entered the office, pulled off my coat, kicked my shoes off, and sauntered over to Danny. I ran my hands over his chest and dropped them down to the belt buckled over his designer jeans. Working the buckle open, I started to unbutton his jeans when the other three men rapidly stood, protesting that they didn't want to see Danny's junk and beat feet out of there.

Danny chuckled and wrapped his arms around me. "Still got a way of clearing the room."

"You know I do," I agreed and stood on tiptoe to kiss him. "Talk dirty to me about cows."

"A sentence I never thought I would hear coming out of your mouth. How was your meeting with Ivan?" Danny asked with a smirk that made me give a love tap to his balls. He jerked back but not in time to avoid the gentle blow.

"Are you testing my fidelity? Because, damn, that one came close. He's hot and I wonder what he'd look like naked," I answered honestly and settled my ass on his desk.

Danny lifted me and had my jeans off in no time flat and set me back down on the edge, spreading my legs. "Tongue wagging?" he asked with a husky tone.

"Cows," I reminded him, feeling the dampness start to spread. Hopefully, I wasn't sitting on any critical papers; they'd be wet now.

"You are not a cow," Danny answered, leaning forward to kiss inside my thigh. "The surveillance footage wasn't tampered with; I can say that with certainty." He turned his head and nipped at the other thigh, higher this time.

I gnawed on my lip for a few seconds to keep myself from jamming his head right between both my thighs and holding it there until I screamed out my delight with his tongue wagging. "Any way you can check the dark web for cattle chatter?"

"You know I have skills," Danny replied with a flick of his tongue.

My thoughts scattered when the second lick happened and I forgot about cows for the two minutes and thirty-eight seconds it took him to turn me into a screaming mass of putty. I was lying over his desk with my chest heaving when I heard his pants hit the floor. I didn't get a chance to refocus my thoughts until fifteen minutes later when we were in the shower cleaning up.

"You want me to plant a bug that will show you chatter about cows?" Danny asked as he soaped up my boobs.

"If it doesn't cross any lines, yeah, that would be helpful. I need to go talk to Mick, too," I answered distractedly and decided to return the favor by washing his balls.

Danny didn't answer for a few seconds other than a long and drawn-out moan. "Damn, woman. No lines crossed for me. I'll do this on barter for you, at no charge. My fee is a weekend away uninterrupted."

That slowed my hands, and I pulled back to step under the spray. We hadn't done the weekend away thing before. The most we had done was an overnight at Danny's place with me dashing off before the sun rose. "Why?"

"Because we work well together and we can have a whole lot more of that shuddering body thing that makes those noises come out of you," Danny growled, pulling me back into him.

It couldn't hurt, right? "Okay. Do it," I told him.

As an answer, he did me again. Against the shower wall this time, though no less gratifying than the time spent on top of his desk. Danny had skills, that was for sure. While we had never agreed to be exclusive, I knew that he was, and he knew that should the opportunity arise, I probably wouldn't be. It was another reason I hadn't moved him from booty call to relationship.

"Headed to Mick's office?" Danny asked me as we dressed.

"Yeah, so thanks for getting my pheromones all worked up and sending me off to a sexy alpha shifter," I replied with a laugh.

"It was my plan all along. It will distract Mick and he'll be more likely to answer those pesky questions you like to bother him with," Danny told me with a swat on the ass. "Now, give me your word that the weekend after you finish this case, you will go away with me."

Shit, he wasn't going to let this go. "Fine, you have my word."

"Say it, Risa. I get an uninterrupted weekend with you when you finish this case," Danny pushed.

"Don't press your luck. I just said I gave you my word." I made my tone match my glare.

"I know you, babe. Say the words,"

Danny's voice lowered again as he crowded into my personal space. His mannerisms were possessive without crossing that line into being demanding in a way that would push me over the edge.

I ground my teeth together and gave him a tight smile. "You aren't playing fair with that attitude; you know I like that." I huffed out an irritated breath. "Fine, when this case is over, I give you my word that we will have an uninterrupted weekend together at a place of your choosing."

Danny crowed out his victory and gave me a searing hot kiss that left me wanting a little more. Reluctant to let myself want more with this man, I pulled away. "Work to do," I replied breathlessly.

I was positive it looked like I was running as I made my way quickly back out to my Jeep. I gunned the engine and kicked up some of the gravel unintentionally and cringed. I yelled sorry out the window and kept going.

Chapter Four

Mick's office was in a pool hall called Blue Balls that bordered Glimmering Rock and Branstone. It served as the pack's clubhouse and an official business frequented by magical and non-magical alike. Mick built the club that way on purpose; Mick's office was on the club's side that rested in Glimmering Rock.

Mick designed it so that the non-magical people wouldn't truly see his office door since it was in the magical territory. It appeared to those people as a storage closet and they tended to look right past it. Ingenious on his part.

I parked in the lot and slid out of the Jeep, waving hello to a medium that lived near me. "Hey, Crowley," I called to him. "How's life treating you?"

"Girl, you got a danger cloud following you," Crowley shot back, his voice slurring a bit.

"Not unusual in my line of work," I told him with a shiver. I hadn't considered that this job would be dangerous. I am not too fond of coincidences, and my magic going wonky wasn't atypical but coupled with the flat tires, it could have been a sign. "Picking up anything specific?"

"Not that I can see," Crowley admitted. "I got a zap when you pulled into the lot that told me danger was nearby. Spirits are quiet. No one is shouting at me today, which I appreciate. I didn't sleep all that well last night. I kept dreaming of cows."

That made me pause mid-step. "Cows? What about them?"

"It's strange because I usually remember, only this time I woke up confused each time." Crowley shook his head, his silvery hair that was sticking out in tufts from under his hat, fluffing up and expanding. "I'd see the cows in what looked like a doctor's office. Who takes cows to a doctor's office?

That's why I thought maybe it was some weird nightmare and not one of the precog dreams. The moos they were making were pathetic sounding and they echoed in my ears when I woke up."

A chill washed over me again, like someone dancing a happy jog on my freshly dug grave. "I'll agree, that's strange. Are you going to be here a while, or are you leaving? I might have some questions for you about those dreams but I need to talk to Mick."

"He's in a pissy mood," Crowley warned me.

"Sounds about right," I muttered and bent over to pat the old man's hand. "Will you still be here?"

"Most likely. I'm on a winning streak. I only came out for some fresh air and one of the spirits that linger here told me to sit outside for a bit. Possibly because I needed to tell you about the danger that's following you or maybe to tell someone about the dreams," Crowley shrugged.

"Okay, we'll talk soon." I straightened

up and headed inside the club. A low growl greeted me from the left and I looked to see the pack's enforcer, Chuck, sitting on a stool watching the door. I gave him one of my patented fuck-off looks and kept walking.

Chuck and I had a history. He hit on me one night several years ago and I took him for a spin. I only ever intended a one-time thing and he got possessive in a bad way. Not like the sexy way that Danny used against me but the stalker way. It ended in a fiasco, the usual Risa way things like that ended. Mick got involved and had to pull rank. Now *that* had been sexy.

I put a little sway into my hips as I passed some of the pool tables and drew a few looks from some bad-boy types, causing one to miss the cue ball. I laughed evilly and kept walking, right down the hall to Mick's office.

I didn't knock. I just opened the door and waltzed in like I had a right to be there. Unfortunately, I caught Mick mid-orgasm. Instead of turning my back to let him finish, I watched him with my cheeks flaming. Not once did the alpha break my stare as he grunted out his release.

However, the woman he was using was about as embarrassed as could be and practically ran from the office, clutching clothes she'd snatched up from the floor to her chest. The door slammed behind her as she fled. I waited for Mick to button his pants up but all he did was tuck himself back in his jeans, leaving them open. Yeah, I looked.

"Risa," Mick drawled. "Want a picture?"

"Not particularly impressed, so that is a no," I retorted, flopping myself into a chair. The bold lie hung in the air between us. "Uh, I wanted to talk to you about Ivan and his cows."

Mick snapped to attention and his temper flared. "I told him it wasn't the pack," Mick snarled at me.

"I wasn't accusing you," I pointed out. "I merely said I wanted to talk to you.

Ivan told me that he had spoken to you about it and has an agreement with you. I am more looking for suggestions on what to search for because it seems to be the timing of the disappearing cows is someone trying to set the pack up to take the fall for it."

Mick relaxed marginally, though I could still feel the snapping anger of his temper close to the surface. I fervently hoped that my magic didn't flare up and cause some mishap to get him right and genuinely pissed off at me. "Ask."

"So, that means you didn't understand that my words were a question without the upturn in my voice to signify that it was a question?" I purposely goaded him.

A slow, cold smile spread across his face. "You think I'm stupid?"

"Did the word stupid come out of my mouth once?" I backed off a little. "What could have gotten into the field undetected and moved quickly enough to not show on the camera?"

"With a potion, a lot of things," Mick

growled. "You already know that. Spit out whatever it is you want to ask."

"Who have you pissed off recently that would want to set you up?" I fired the question at him.

"Probably half the town," Mick admitted with a grin. "To the point of setting me up for a crime, that's a different thing. I'm not sure that I've done anything to warrant that or that anyone in my pack did."

"Grudges?" I pressed him.

"Possibly. That will require a bit of time for me to think about; I think best during sex. Want a ride?" Mick stood and stretched, exposing the opened jeans and happy trail that tapered down his ripped abs to the hardening pole I glimpsed earlier.

"No. You can't handle me," I spouted off. "I was taken care of earlier, anyway."

"You only think you were satisfied. I can show you a different world," Mick stepped closer to me. "The smell is driving me nuts; you could have at least showered."

"I did. But I had another round in the

shower," I offered up lamely. The unbuttoned jeans were as distracting to me as the smell of sex was to him. "Maybe you smell yourself."

"Nice try but no. Want to stick your face down here and smell?" Mick held his hand open in an inviting gesture.

Verbal sparring with him was fun, yet I found myself at a loss for words for once. "There is no one you can think of right off the bat?" I hoped the change of subject worked.

Mick chuckled. "Point to me. I'm sure if I thought about it, I could come up with names. Do you honestly believe that someone is targeting me at the same time they are stealing cows? It's not like those are easy to hide. They have to be going somewhere."

I already knew that. "How about you come up with some names for me. Leave the rest of the investigating to me."

"Lucky for you that you are nice to look at, Risa. Not many people get away with talking to me like that, much less walking in on me and cutting my fun short. I've had some of my people watching the new guy in town; he smells off to me. Wiley, I think his name is. The day he moved here, he made it a point to come by and sought me out, told me that he wanted to be friendly with all the leaders in the city," Mick freely offered up. "Yet, I didn't see him seeking anyone else out or any of the other leaders visit him."

"You've been watching since the day he moved here?" I asked dumbfounded. I usually had a better pulse on things.

"Oh yeah. Rich guy moving into town and seeking me out? That raises suspicion with me." Mick nodded. "He has shifter blood, a race I'm not familiar with."

"He's a shifter?" I echoed, sounding dumb.

"Best as I can tell," Mick nodded again.

It didn't sit right with me; I'd have picked up on Wiley being a shifter. His scent was different; I *had* noticed that. It was eerily similar to mine in the mixed way it came across. To me, that meant he wasn't a shifter, or at least, not a full-blooded shifter. Strange that Mick would miss that.

"Anything else standing out about him?" I shifted my stance slightly and crossed my arms, drawing Mick's eyes to my boobs.

"I don't trust him," Mick replied distractedly with a smirk on his face. "I think he's dangerous. Most would take that as a warning that they shouldn't trust him either. Yet, I know you'll do whatever you want."

Mick moved and started stalking towards me, pushing me to the door. "You done with me now?" I couldn't help the snark.

"Don't get killed until I get a chance to sample the goods, darlin'," Mick bent over and hotly whispered in my ear.

Reflexively, my hand shot out and cupped his junk, squeezing it. "Keep dreaming." I turned on my heel and strode out of the office, leaving the stunned alpha werewolf standing there with his mouth open.

I'm sure my face was flaming and I didn't care. Something was alluring about the pack alpha. It was more than the size of his junk emblazoned on the palm of my hand. Alluring or not, he was also a cocky asshole. His warning about Wiley being dangerous hung in the back of my mind.

Chapter Five

I didn't have any more information on Ivan's case than I had before I came here. I had another mystery I wanted to solve. My instincts told me that there might be a connection between the two, but I couldn't see it yet. It wouldn't behoove me to haul off and accuse the new resident of a crime I had no evidence to support.

So what exactly did I have? I knew six female cows had disappeared without a trace. Video surveillance of the grounds showed no trespassers and a slight blip on one of the feeds. A new guy moved into town asking about invisibility potions. A son that worked in the black market and involved another son in whatever new scheme was afoot involving an ex. Invisible fingers were pointing towards the wolf pack. Tech guy looked at videos and they haven't been tampered with at all.

I wrote each of those things down in a bulleted list and stared at it while sitting in the driver's seat of my Jeep. Under the last bullet point, I noted that I spoke with Mick and spotted no signs that he was lying to me. Under the new guy bullet, I wrote that his scent was muddled and Mick felt he was dangerous. I didn't believe my sons were involved but I had to look into that angle as well, in all fairness.

As for Danny's part, I knew there was no deception there. To not appear on a camera, someone would have had to have used a potion for invisibility, or maybe hyper-speed, and that's what the blip was. The other thing my brain huffed up the side of implication mountain to trip on was what if there was a portal on the property that no one ever stumbled over?

The thought prompted me to turn the page in my notebook and make another bullet list. Who can create portals? Where do they go? Is this a new portal or was it something that existed previously and was re-found by someone? Who would have access to the portal? Why take cows? That last thought led to, what if the cows just walked through by accident?

I tapped my pen on my teeth, staring at the side of the building, lost in thought about the possibilities that this might all be some weird fluke that the cows themselves tripped through. It wasn't a stretch but how did that tie in with the moon phases? That's what turned the whole debacle on its side.

A portal was highly plausible, as well as cows finding it by accident. The disappearances on moon phases were not, which told me that there was a person behind this, and they were trying to deflect attention away from themselves by throwing it on the wolf pack.

Mick, the well-endowed prick, wasn't altogether liked but everyone respected him. He kept his pack in line, behaving, and treated them fairly. He didn't use his position to bully his way into getting things, nor was he the most powerful leader. Mick regarded the law, upheld it, and meted out punishments when deserved.

The bear clan was more likely to step outside the boundaries of the law than the wolves were. For that matter, so were the wyverns. The unicorns had a few run-ins with the wolves a few years back. I was willing to stake my reputation on this having zero to do with the wolves. For all I knew, it could be one of the humans that resided here and was in tune with the supernatural.

I sighed then immediately almost wet my pants when someone tapped on the window. So much for situational awareness, I hadn't even heard the crunching of footsteps on the gravel. Plus, I hadn't locked the Jeep door behind me when I got in. Not smart.

My head whipped around to see my middle son's smiling face pressed against the window. "Hi, Mom! I was driving by on my way to work and saw your Jeep parked here and thought I'd stop to say hello. Sorry I missed your call but I was with someone. I met someone!" Gage crowed and stepped back from the window so I could open the door and climb out.

I hugged him and then moved to lean against the Jeep. "You met someone?" I asked with raised eyebrows. Gage was always meeting someone. It was that selkie blood of his. Selkie's had incredible seductive powers yet didn't maintain long-term relationships well. As evidenced by Gage's father and now Gage.

"Yes, I did! He's amazing! My first satyr." Gage threw his arms around me again. "I met him at work. He came into the restaurant to have dinner and asked to meet the chef. It was love at first sight." Gage looked around the parking lot, "What are you doing here?"

Interesting and not surprising. Gage was a good-looking man and that's not my mother's bias talking. It also didn't hurt that Gage was a very well-known chef with unparalleled skills when it came to creating mouthwatering dishes.

"I'm working on a case. And congratulations, I hope the relationship works out for you." I patted his arm. "Do you know what your brothers are up to lately? Have you heard any rumors about cows? Black market meat or anything like that?"

Gage frowned. "That's disturbing and the answer is a resounding no. I haven't talked to Gavin recently but I did talk to Jameson a couple of days ago and he said he was helping Gavin with a project and left it at that. Do you still want me to probe?"

"No, Gavin will know I put you up to it and I don't want to create tension. Jameson will spill if I can get him cornered. What's on tonight's menu?" I asked him. Not that I could afford to eat at his restaurant.

"I'm going to marinate some portobellos in a wine sauce, sauté them, then stuff them with a seared veal and some fresh herbs," Gage told me with a crooked smile.

"Sounds rich," I quipped, playing with words.

"Want me to save you one?" Gage laughed, knowing I was referring to the flavor as well as the price tag.

"No. I'm sure it will be excellent but I'm not crazy about mushrooms or veal," I told him as I righted myself. "Get going. I don't want you to be late. If you hear anything else, let me know."

"Love you, Mom. We'll do dinner soon so you can meet Arion." Gage kissed my cheek and climbed back into his fancy Mercedes and zoomed off. He'd done well for himself and I was proud of him.

"Arion," I muttered as I got back in the Jeep. "A satyr." Maybe this time would be different, who knows. His last girlfriend only wanted him for meals and sex. At least Gage was an equal opportunity dater and didn't define his sexuality as the humans did; added bonus, he was luckier in love than I was, though that's not saying much.

Before I took off to my next location, I pulled my phone from my pocket and called Danny. "Hey," I greeted him when he picked up. "Do me a favor and look at those videos again and tell me if the cows are stationary when they disappear or are they moving around a bit."

"Got it," Danny agreed distractedly. "I'm working on your worm bug right now. I'll text you about the cows."

"Thanks, you're the best," I told him in my sweetest voice, which only made him laugh.

Hanging up, I decided that my next course of action was to check out Ivan's field. It carried some risk, yet I had to consider that Ivan hadn't disappeared and he had been in his fields. I shrugged to myself. Visiting another area via portal couldn't be all that bad, could it? I mean, if it happened, I'd probably find the cows, then case solved.

Chapter Six

Ivan, hi, it's Risa," I greeted the sexy farmer when he answered his cell phone. "I was wondering if it would be okay if I stopped by to look at the field?"

"Sure, I'm home," Ivan replied with a smile in his voice. "Should I cook us up some dinner?" he flirted with me.

I swallowed a groan at my stupid no dating client rules. I blame Mick for getting me all stirred up again after my sessions with Danny. I *was* hungry but I couldn't cross those lines I drew. "I appreciate the offer and if you are offering a raincheck, I'll take that."

Ivan's rich chuckle tickled my ears. "A woman with unbreakable morals, I like it. I'll see you when you get here. Do you need the address?"

I was pretty sure I knew where he lived, however, better safe than sorry. "Yes, please. I'm not in the office."

Ivan rattled off his address, I wrote it in my notebook, and we hung up. My conscience ate at me, and I sent a quick text to Danny, letting him know where I was going. I rationalized it in the back of my head, telling myself it was for safety reasons and not because I felt guilty for going to Ivan's. It was work, that's all. I rolled my eyes at myself and got the Jeep started. I wasn't in a relationship.

I considered driving by the city's new resident while I was out to check out his place myself. I didn't want to do that alone; I talked myself out of it. If Mick didn't trust him, he was right, and I should exercise caution. Especially since I already had an encounter with him in the black market of all places.

I tried to shake off the frazzled feeling that was hanging over me. I wanted to blame it on the afternoon nookie, and I knew it wasn't that. It was the combination of Braxton, my sons, a weekend away with

Danny, Ivan, and the possible chance meeting with Wiley earlier. I was used to a lot going on, only not in my personal life like that.

Thoroughly distracted while driving, shame on me, I didn't notice the fancy sports car practically crawling up my tailpipe until the engine revved and drew my attention. With a glance in my rearview mirror, I spotted the mysterious Wiley with a smirk on his face; he was that close.

I felt tempted to hit the brakes but my Jeep was as much my baby as my kids were. Instead, I smiled sweetly and flipped him off. I saw him throw his head back in laughter and then he sped around me, waving as he passed.

Now I hoped he was involved in this cow thing somehow, only to give me a reason to send the police after him. I didn't care if he had enough money to buy them off, which he probably did; it would still inconvenience him. I had a natural-born talent for pissing men off and Wiley just moved himself to the number one spot on my list. Cocky ass-clown.

Ten minutes of plotting against Wiley later, I pulled into Ivan's driveway for the ranch. He owned a large tract of well-maintained land. Cows freely roamed the fields with a scenic view complete with green rolling hills in the background. At the back of the property lie the dairy barns, a silo, and some other buildings I didn't want to know about lest I suddenly find myself not wanting ever to eat a burger again.

I parked next to a bright blue pickup truck and got out, looking around. It was a nice setup but the smell of cow shit would get to me if I lived here. I could tolerate it for the length of a quickie. The thought popped into my head before I could stop it and I laughed to myself, shaking my head. Honestly, I wasn't that quick or easy to drop my pants.

"What's so funny?" Ivan asked, walking up.

"Random thoughts of hook-ups that

appear in my mind," I told him truthfully. "Want to direct me to where the livestock disappeared? Were they all in the same field?"

"I'm digging your Jeep; she's a beauty. And I can totally understand why Danny is lost on you," Ivan laughed. "I'll do you one better than directing you. I'll take you there myself. We can take the cart."

The cart turned out to be a Polaris RZR, my first time being in one of those. I could have fun with it, though it probably wasn't a great idea in the cow fields. Silently, I got in and kept my mouth shut while he drove us through the fields. It seemed like we were going for miles. I was glad he was driving and I wasn't walking through pastures of cow shit.

"Okay, all the disappearances happened in this backfield but not all in the same spot. Was there a theory that you were working on?" Ivan asked as he brought the cart to a stop.

"Possibly," I admitted slowly, drawing

out the word. "How much do you know about the magical world?"

"My mom was a mage. I know a fair amount but I got none of the magical D.N.A., unfortunately. There are times I think it would be useful, though I am not bitter about it. My life is good, and I've done alright. Why do you ask?" Ivan turned in his seat, so his body faced mine.

"The thought that there might be a portal here struck me. I have Danny looking at the videos again and I wanted to scout out the area," I stuck with the truth. "There are different types of portals, and it's possible there was one here before you came here or that someone opened one and left it."

A stunned look crossed Ivan's face. "Can't say I considered that. How will you know?"

I laughed lightly. "Hopefully, by feeling the magic of it and not accidentally stepping through one to an unknown location."

Ivan's nervous laughter was tight and

fear lined his eyes. "Okay then. I'll trail behind you given that answer. I guess, at least if you vanish into thin air, I'll know why. If that happens, how do I get you back?"

"Don't follow me in, that's for sure. Call Danny if that happens," I instructed him. "Which way?"

Ivan silently pointed and watched while I climbed out of the cart and gazed around. He followed my actions and kept his distance. I could see that the thought of a portal scared him. Honestly, it scared me too. Only because I didn't want to end up in some other realm with creatures ready to eat me, maybe I would mind less if my magic wasn't unpredictable.

My phone vibrated in my pocket, causing me to flinch; I pulled it out and saw the text from Danny. *Cows were in motion.*

Okay, that helped. That means the cows most likely walked or were led into a portal if there was one here. I slid the phone back into my pocket and watched my step. My shoes might not be designer shoes but that didn't mean I wanted them smelling like a cow pasture either.

I headed in the direction that Ivan had pointed and the tingle washed over me that told me magic was present. I held my hand up to halt Ivan and tried to feel it out. "There's magic here or someone has recently used magic here. I can feel it on my skin," I whispered harshly.

My nerves felt like they were vibrating; it was so thick. I slowed my pace, so I didn't step through a portal, then stopped. I studied the ground around me without moving and found a stick. Bending over, I snatched it up and held it out in front of me like a sword. I glanced back and saw Ivan mimicking me and stifled a snort of laughter. We looked ridiculous.

I began moving again at a snail's pace, alternately watching my step and the stick. If part of that stick vanished, I would know the portal was in front of me. Hopefully, it wasn't one that would suck me in like a black hole. Portals weren't a topic I was overly educated in; I only knew the basics.

Creating a portal took an immense amount of magic, which helped me narrow down the list of suspects to those with a deep pool of power at their disposal. Most commonly made by fae, mages, or witches, though other races could produce the magic needed.

"If I get pulled onto a foreign planet, we might have to rediscuss your fee," Ivan called out feebly.

I snickered, "Relax. It will get me before it gets you. Have you moved your cows out of this area?"

"I did after I got home today," Ivan replied cautiously. "Figured it was a wise move and now I'm glad I did. If there is a portal here, can it be taken down?"

"Yeah. It might cost a pretty penny, though. It's not something I can do and I'll provide you a list of trusted people after we figure this out. Correction, after *I* figure it out. You don't have to follow me. You can stay back with the cart," I told him, turning to look behind me.

"Feels like the manly thing to do, you know, making sure you are okay and all," Ivan muttered warily. "Your balls might be bigger than mine."

Maintaining professionalism wasn't always a strong suit of mine and I'm not quite sure how I managed not to burst into laughter at his admission. I turned back around quickly before Ivan saw the amusement on my face and resumed my forward walk.

It didn't take long for the stick to find the portal. My skin felt like there were thousands of creepy crawly insects flowing over it. My curiosity was going to be the death of me someday. I badly wanted to stick my head through and see what was on the other side. I'd never been through a portal before.

"Don't come closer," I warned Ivan. "The portal is in front of me."

I threw the stick into the portal to see if the magic's feel changed when something entered it. I halfway expected the branch to be lobbed back at me. I jolted a bit when I felt Ivan at my back. He reached around me and jabbed his stick in the direction I had thrown mine and gasped as he saw the end vanish.

"You don't listen well, do you?" I giggled and took the stick from him. "Back up a few feet. I'm going to try and figure out how big this thing is."

"Fearless. Danny's words didn't do you justice. He underplayed you." Ivan shook his head and backed up.

I wasn't fearless. My heart was hammering out a bizarre rhythm in my chest. Granted, it might be that excited fear but it was still fear. I inched closer to the portal and swept the stick from side to side until I felt it hit the unseen edge of the invisible opening.

I bent over and made a mark in the ground to signify that it was the left end. To be sure, I moved the stick around on the other side of it and there was nothing there. I returned to the task and did the same thing until I found the right side and marked that.

To satisfy my curiosity, I moved the stick up until I found the top. I didn't have a way to mark that, and it became evident to me that two cows side by side and stacked on each other could fit through this portal. It was good sized.

"I've been here for ten years. How is it that I've not lost any employees or myself in that thing?" Ivan asked with his eyes widened, looking like saucers.

"Maybe on some level, you can feel the magic of the portal and it repels you," I suggested, not entirely sure. "Maybe you are incredibly lucky. Got any wire fencing or stuff to circle around this to keep people out?"

Ivan blinked at me a few times, mouth hanging open. Finally, he shook himself out of the stupor and he pulled his phone from his pocket and called someone. "I'm in the far-field. Can you bring out the spare chicken wire fencing and some of the pink ribbon we use to mark the electric fences? You'll see the cart; stop there."

While he was relaying directions to whoever he was talking to, I marked the spot in front where the stick vanished. I moved around to the other side of the portal to see if this was a double-sided thing. To my utter shock, I couldn't see through it. Ivan was no longer in my sight.

"Don't move," I yelled out to Ivan. I waved the stick in front of me and sucked in my breath when it disappeared. "Good to know," I muttered and began making the same marks over here.

I made my way around it to where Ivan had frozen in place, making me laugh again. "Won't marking it like this make it obvious we know about this if there is a person behind this thing?" Ivan waved his hands around in front of him.

"Yeah, it will. I plan on spending the night out here to see if anyone comes through it at night. I guess if your offer of dinner is still on the table, you can bring it out here to me," I shrugged at the astonished look on his face.

Ivan pulled his phone back out of his pocket silently and called someone while he stared at me. "Hey, bring camping supplies with you. Tent, bag, pad, extra rope, several bottles of water, flashlight, and make sure the gate is closed behind you so the cattle can't get back into this field. Thanks."

Chapter Seven

Ivan hadn't argued with me, which I was thankful for, and I knew he wanted to. Solving his problem was what he hired me for and that's what I was going to do. I needed to observe the portal and if someone came through I had every intention of detaining them.

Now, Danny, he'd argued. He slightly wigged out that there was a portal on the property that no one knew existed. I suspect that someone knew and probably someone that worked for Ivan. No one might have ever run directly into the portal but since his cows started disappearing, I'm guessing that someone discovered it.

As much as I wanted it to be Wiley, Ivan told me he hadn't seen the man on his property. Wiley's search for invisibility potions said to me that if he had been using them, Ivan wouldn't have seen him. My gut told me this wasn't Wiley, though.

We'd set up the tent off to the side under a few trees to provide me with a little cover if someone or something did come through. I already knew Ivan's camera covered this area and my hope wasn't that he was gluing himself to the security screen to watch me. Not only would it make peeing outside more challenging but it would give away my plan to go through the portal.

It made me question my sanity, sure, but the thrill of trying something new pulled at me and I rationalized it that it would help me solve this case and possibly get back Ivan's cows. Yep, total bullshit. I knew it. I was more than aware that I wanted to say I'd traveled somewhere via a portal. Who wouldn't? Come on, that's incredibly cool.

I also know that's why Danny argued with me so vehemently. He knew I was going to do it. I didn't even need to say anything, and if I knew Danny, he'd already hacked Ivan's cameras and was watching me as well. The thought made me roll my eyes again.

I checked my watch and kept my eyes on the portal for a few hours without moving my body. I wanted it to look like I was asleep. From my position, I could see both sides of the mystery portal, and the tingle of magic was a little less. However, I could still feel it.

So when the air changed and felt charged with volatile electricity, I noticed, and my eyes didn't shift away from the portal. Visibly you wouldn't know something was happening. Audibly I heard a faint crackle and pop sound, and then the air went back to normal.

I had no idea what it meant but I suspected that someone came through because I didn't feel alone. I feigned sleep with my eyes cracked open enough to see. Anyone who was watching wouldn't know that anything changed or that I was on high alert. There was nothing in this field for anyone to steal other than me and they wouldn't find me as docile as a cow. Hopefully.

My luck was holding out because my

arm was down by my side and I was able to use my fingers to pat my hip and reassure myself that I had my knife tucked into my hidden pocket and with the way I was lying, the gun I had tucked into my waistband was pressing into my back.

I kept my breathing even and stayed as still as possible, which was a direct argument with my cells screaming at me to move and do something. Take up a defense, fight, seek, something other than lying here doing nothing.

"Fuck!" I heard someone whisper harshly and the chicken wire moving.

Confirmation I wasn't alone and someone at the very least was using an invisibility potion or they could make themselves invisible. Personally, I hoped the guy was using the potion, which would mean they aren't as powerful as they thought they were. Or so that was what my brain was reasoning out.

Inactivity wasn't something I excelled at, and I was itching to make a move. Only, where? Invisibility didn't mean silence and I was doing my best to listen to see if I could narrow down where the person was. The problem was the grass was dewy and not making its typical crunching sound. If I could turn on the flashlight, I could look for footsteps, though that would give me away in a split second.

I shouldn't have worried; I was noticed by the telltale hand on my ankle yanking me right out of the tent. Glad I'd had the foresight to wrap the exceptionally long rope around my hand and wrist and anchored it to the tree behind me, I held tight to it.

"Hey," I shouted. "Let me go!" I struggled and kicked weakly, no sense in giving my strength away. I wanted every upper hand I could get. I hoped someone, Danny or Ivan, was watching to see me getting dragged by nothing and that they heard me shout.

I received no response other than the hand around my ankle, tightening to an almost painful grip. I could gauge where the man was by my positioning and the hold on me, yet I didn't fight back too much. I needed to see who was behind this at the very least.

I didn't expect the violent kick to my midsection that left me without air for more than a few seconds. That had been uncalled for and quite painful. However, it worked as a distraction against the magic that began crawling over me the closer we got to the portal opening.

"Stop damaging the goods, asshole," I ground out when I could speak again. Not sure how whoever this was missed the rope trailing behind me, but I wasn't going to look a gift horse in the mouth. I was going to beat the shit out of this douche who thought they could get away with kicking me, though.

Too late, I realized we were at the portal entrance as the flash of pink ribbon crossed my vision. I hadn't even heard or seen the chicken wire move this time. What the hell? My magic started stirring and an aggressive bolt of something slammed through my organs. Whatever the mixed bag of genetics was inside me reacted with the portal.

It felt like an explosion tore through me. I heard a body landing somewhere away from me and I became disoriented. Shit. I better not be stuck wherever I was. That wouldn't end well for anyone stuck here with me.

I did a mental checklist; all my arms and legs were present, fingers and toes could wiggle. I could feel my gun and the rope. I shifted with a groan and felt for my knife; it was there. I forced my eyes open next. Wherever I was, it was dark, just like at Ivan's farm. I could breathe, which meant there was oxygen. Likewise, I was on the ground, so there was gravity.

Conclusion: I was somewhere on earth. Therefore, I wasn't stuck. I reached for my cell phone and saw that I had no service. It could be that whatever happened when I went through the portal ruined something inside of it. All I had to do was find a way to call Danny and he'd get me home.

Satisfied that I wasn't on a strange planet or realm, I sat up and rubbed my stomach where I'd gotten kicked. *Luck, stick with me,* I thought and pushed myself to stand. I tugged on the rope and was disappointed to see that I couldn't tell if it was intact or not; it was too dark.

A loud screech sounded from in front of me and I involuntarily stepped back. That didn't sound human or like any animal that I'd ever heard. My magic rolled under the surface of my skin and a tiny fission of fear cracked my calm facade. Doubt about being on earth crept into my head.

Instinct had me throwing my hands out in front of me, and something slammed into me, shoving me backward. Wonky magic shot out of my hands in the form of a fireball and what it illuminated made me pause and my jaw unhinged itself as it dropped open.

Nope. Not on earth. It looked like I was in a Jules Verne world mixed with something Wes Craven would come up with for a horror movie. Those four seconds of light were long enough for my fear to grow. I didn't think there would be any calling Danny. That damn rope better be intact.

"You bitch!" a man screamed at me.

Well, there *was* a human here, the one who took me, I assumed. "You dragged me here unwillingly and *I'm* the bitch?" I retorted. "You need to rethink that."

I heard a moo in the distance; the cow didn't sound distressed, not that I would know the difference. I was guessing because I didn't appreciate the thought that a cow was suffering. The distant sound meant I'd have to cross who knows how far in the forest of trees that looked like they had teeth. Wait, could I be in the fae lands? They had scary shit.

Movement sounded from my right, and I pivoted, raising my arms again. This time a wall of shimmering purple light emanated from me and sat in front of me. The dude wasn't invisible here or had something I'd done make that happen? Whatever it was, he crashed into the wall with his face, which made me laugh. Priorities, laughter kept me sane.

"Ouch, that had to hurt," I called out snidely. "Where are we?"

"Fuck off, bitch. You ruined my paycheck and probably destroyed the portal!" the guy glared at me with blood dripping from his rapidly swelling nose.

"Okay, thanks for your assistance. I'll be paying you back for that kick, by the way. For now, I'll go retrieve the cows and make my way home," I casually replied. Luckily the heavy sarcasm in my voice masked the growing fear.

"They'll kill you," my kidnapper snapped with an evil grin.

"Many have tried; they all failed," I batted my eyes at him. "Including you."

Chapter Eight

All I could do was hope that the rope was long enough for me to find the cows. There was no chance I was letting it go; it was my lifeline at the moment. I picked my way gingerly through vegetation that felt like it was alive. Not in the way that plants are living on earth but alive like a sentient being. I had little doubt that everything here could be lethal.

I didn't know what magic had come from me with that purple wall but the ass-clown who brought me here was trapped by it. When he moved, the wall did too. It was impressive and I wished that I could produce that voluntarily.

Now I was inching my way towards what I assumed was a building. A chimney or something that passed for one was belching a foul-smelling smoke. It looked like a mud hut that primitive people of earth would have built for shelter. Only the mud appeared to be moving like a waterfall. Strange was an understatement.

Sometime in the past ten minutes, I had decided I wasn't in fae lands. I honestly had no clue where I was, and I felt trapped in a dream-like state. The one thing I was sure of was I wanted to go home. If I didn't manage to round up the cows now, it meant I'd have to come back. I didn't think my entrance would be as subtle as it was this time. If feeling like you exploded was subtle.

Bioluminescent plants were around the building, emitting an odd colored light that was almost red in appearance. If it weren't for those plants and the purple wall, I'd be utterly lost. Those were the two light sources. Otherwise, I'd be entirely dependent on the rope around my wrist.

I swallowed a girly scream that threatened to erupt from my throat when a Cujo looking Cerberus type dog appeared fifteen feet in front of me. "Nice doggy thingy," I crooned. "Please tell me you are a pet and friendly."

"No, I'm not a pet or friendly," the creature answered me.

Color me shocked senseless. "Uh, hi," I finally spit out. "Are you here to hurt me?"

"I haven't decided. How is it you understand me?" the speaking freak dog asked.

"You aren't speaking English?" I paused. "Where am I?"

"What *are* you?" the thing asked back.

"A magical humanoid being with mixed blood," I answered hotly, slightly offended. I reached behind me and gripped the gun. I didn't want to shoot the pup but I would if I needed to.

"You are like the one you trapped back there?" the talking dog sat back on its haunches and pointed with a paw.

I scoffed, "Hardly. That idiot is beneath me on the food chain. Tell me how to get the cows back. And your name and where I am and if I can go back?"

"You are a demanding creature," his tone changed to one more threatening than it already had been. A series of sounds came from him that sounded like a cross between beeping, choking on marshmallows, and sneezing.

"What the fuck?" I spouted off.

"I don't know that word. I told you my name and your location," the dog creature growled out.

"Uh, okay. I'll call you Cujo since that didn't translate and this place will be christened WTF world," I drawled, wondering if I was pushing my luck. "Where are the cows and can I get them out of here, back to where I came from?"

"Are those the smelly things that emit some disgusting form of gas?" Cujo stood on his hind legs and I found myself looking up into one of his three heads.

"Yeah, those. Will I be able to use the portal to get back?" I asked again, unnerved by this creature.

"It used only to work one way unless

you had the charm to activate it from this world. Then you came through and now it's open." Cujo shrugged and waved his arm behind him. "Your creatures are over there. Scientists are doing something with them. The worthless one like you back there has been selling them."

"Cow trafficking. I've heard it all," I snorted. "Great. I'll be retrieving the smelly things and get out of your hair. I'll figure out how to disable the portal once I'm home. That way, your world won't be wrecked by people from mine." Crowley's dreams flitted across my mind.

Cujo gave a huff of disdain and I swear all three heads rolled their eyes at me. "Do what you will. I'm merely an underpaid and underappreciated guard for the scientists. I typically kill whoever comes through."

I shuddered, thankful my leprechaun luck was holding. "Much obliged for not killing me."

"For now. You are pleasing to look

at." Cujo moved off to the side and motioned me forward. "I can't say what the scientists will do."

Great, I thought. I followed Cujo to the flowing mud building, trying to process everything that had happened up to this moment. It was pointless since I understood none of it. I was in an alien world, talking to a three-headed dog that guarded scientists who bought trafficked cows from Earth. *What?*

"Through there." Cujo opened the door.

I wanted to plug my nose. I walked past Cujo and into the dark building, managing not to touch anything. The world had to be toxic to create three-headed talking dogs. Danny might not put out if I sprouted another head.

I came upon another scene that froze my already paralyzed brain. Three millipede looking creatures were in the room wearing lab coats and swimming goggles, extracting milk and blood from the cows. No wonder

Crowley hadn't remembered much about his dreams. There were no words to accurately describe the *what the fuck* thoughts flying through my head. Ivan's case shot to the top of my strangest list. And I'd seen some pretty weird shit.

"Hey!" I shouted, startling the hundreds of arms that were doing whatever constituted as science here and made them stop. Goggled bug-eyes stared at me in fascination, thoroughly creeping me out. "Those cows don't belong to you!"

The room filled with the sounds of nervous cows and that beeping, choking, sneezing sound as all three bug-people started making sounds. Why could I understand Cujo and not these things? Magic prickled against my skin and I didn't want to hurt the cows, so I drew my pistol and leveled it at the head of the closest bug.

"Don't kill them," Cujo said from behind me. "I'd have to defend them and hurt you."

What I could only assume was a

conversation ensued and a sharp yank on the rope had me flying backward through the air, right into Cujo, who caught me by my boobs, of course. Add groped by an alien creature to my list of experiences.

"Hands off." I pushed away from him. I was glowing with magic. "Tell them those cows were stolen and didn't belong to the man who sold them. I'll be taking them with me."

I plugged my ears to block talking since it was giving me a headache and moved to the cows. Removing the very earthly looking modern medical equipment they were using, I tried to figure out how to get six cows to follow me. I had no herding experience. I couldn't even get my kids to follow me.

"They would like me to explain to you that they are extracting genetic material from the creatures to blend with another to create one animal that they can use as surf and turf. I am unsure what that means but those are their words, not mine," Cujo stated, sounding confused. "Something about duplicating a sustenance the other brought with him."

Dumbfounded once again, I failed to notice the rope attached to me was pulling tight again. Knocked off balance, I startled the cow next to me and almost got stepped on by a hoof. I unwound the rope and began to weave it over the cow's heads, hoping there was enough. The next yank made the first tethered cow move towards the door.

"Yes!" I crowed. My skin was still luminescent and wasn't helping the nervous cow situation. "Cujo, help me," I pleaded.

"I think I'd rather observe," Cujo replied drolly.

"Asshole," I muttered, working fast, trying to wind the rope around cow necks, hoping I didn't choke them out. With the last one finished, I followed, holding the remaining short end of the rope/harness next to the cow.

"What is surf and turf?" Cujo asked, trailing after me.

"Food," I told him. "Your scientists are trying to create an animal to harvest for food. Some weird hybrid cross between a sea creature and a land creature, if what you told me is correct."

"I don't lie," Cujo sounded cross.

I stopped responding to his questions and prodded the cows as best as I could. I wanted out of this place. It felt like it took forever for the cows to meander their way back to the portal and I wondered how long I had been here. Too long was the immediate answer that popped in my head.

Looking at my still trapped kidnapper, who was sleeping now, I wondered if I could bring him back with me and how I would get around the purple wall. First, my bigger problem was getting the lead cow to walk into the portal that obviously made them skittish. Not that I could blame them.

I tugged on the rope in a desperate attempt and hoped there was someone on the other end to pull back. It took a few minutes of me trying but it eventually worked and the first cow mooed its unhappiness with the situation. I got behind the old lady and shoved with all my might and she finally took the first step forward into nothingness.

One cow rescued, I sighed. I was grateful that the rest were inclined to follow the first, and the heifers, one by one, entered the portal. As the last one took a step forward, I turned to the sleeping thief.

Reaching my hand out, I tentatively touched the purple wall and watched amazed as it disintegrated at the contact. Interesting. The strange world had an odd effect on my magic. No longer hesitating, I grabbed the man by his neck and cracked the butt of my pistol against his skull, then threw him bodily into the portal.

Turning to look behind me once, I saw Cujo among the trees, watching me. I raised my hand in farewell and turned to the portal. Not wanting to wait around to be kept captive by a three-headed talking dog and his millipede goggle-wearing bosses, I entered the portal.

Once again, magic crackled painfully against my skin but it spat me out into broad daylight and a stunned Ivan and Danny. Not caring that they were looking at me, I dropped to my knees and kissed the grass.

"Damn, Risa! Are you okay?" Danny broke out of his stupor and raced over to me, hauling me to my feet.

"As far as I know. That asshole there kicked me in the gut. Fucker might have bruised some ribs." I looked over at Ivan, "Do you know him?"

"Sure do, he's one of my ranch hands," Ivan muttered darkly. "He's the one who took my cows?"

I broke down into hysterical laughter, no longer able to contain my happiness at being back. "Yeah. The asshole was trafficking the cows. Might want to have a vet check them out. The cows, not him."

"So, um, this new skin color you are sporting is different, kind of hot," Danny said into my ear. "Want to explain?"

"Later. I want a shower." I patted Danny's ass and looked back at Ivan, "What time is it? We can debrief later."

"Risa, you've been gone almost two weeks," Ivan sputtered out. "We can debrief in the morning."

Stunned, I looked back at where the portal was, sitting sight unseen. "Uh, well, I wasn't expecting that." I checked my phone; seeing a strong signal, I called the mages that I knew who specialized in portals and arranged for them to come and shut it down immediately. "I'll wait until they get here, then so long. We can meet at my office in the morning. Not before ten."

Ivan nodded numbly, then called his vet to check the cows. "Thank you."

Chapter Nine

All three of my sons came to dinner that night, each one worried in their way. Part of me wondered if the reason they came was to eat the dinner Gage was bringing. I'd do things I didn't want to do for one of his meals.

Jameson stuck close to my side the whole night and ended up spilling his involvement with potions, which didn't make Gavin too happy, but he felt shaken up that the guy he was working with forced me through a portal and assaulted me.

Mother's instinct was telling me there was more to it than that little involvement with the cow trafficker but I was too tired to push him on it. There was time; besides, Jameson would end up spilling the rest of it if Gavin didn't succumb to my angry mom stare.

I slept like a rock that night and

texted Danny to let him know I was okay and was heading to meet Ivan. I splashed some water on my face and was finishing getting dressed when he responded.

I'll be there. Don't forget that we have a weekend date this weekend. Portal is closed; I made sure of it.

Damn, I *had* forgotten about the weekend away with him. As for him sitting in on the meeting, I didn't care. He'd been a part of it and as long as Ivan didn't mind, neither did I. It would also be amusing to see the look on his face when he found out the reason the ranch hand took the cows.

Grabbing one of the muffins that Gage had left for me, I headed to the office. The rundown building had never looked so good after the flowing mud smelly one I was inside. I huffed out an irritated breath at the mail piled up on the floor of past due bills and I marveled that I had been gone for two weeks. It felt like only a couple of hours.

Shaking my head, I gathered up the mail and stuffed it in my top drawer and lowered myself into my desk chair only to have it similarly eject me to what it had done when Ivan appeared in my life.

Growling, I stood to the sound of laughter. "Is this a pattern?" Ivan asked.

Rolling my eyes, I yanked the offending furniture back behind my desk and jammed my ass into it. "Seems to be. Danny said he was coming; you okay with that?"

"Yep. Danny freaked out when you disappeared. Can't wait to hear this." Ivan sat down and crossed his arms.

"You don't have to wait long. I'm here," Danny announced, entering the office and gently closing the door behind him. He set a thumb drive down on my desk. "The video of you disappearing is on there. Thought you might want it for any files you keep on cases."

Danny was the only thoughtful warlock that I knew. I tucked the drive into my desk drawer on top of the bills. "Thanks. You guys ready for some crazy shit?"

They nodded and I launched into a

detailed account of what had happened. It amused me to no end, the disbelief written across the men's faces as they listened. By the time I finished, Danny appeared unhappy and Ivan looked like I had told him his dick talked to me and told me its secrets.

Ivan blinked a few times, then pulled out his checkbook and wrote me a check, padding it nicely. "Including hazard pay. I was hoping to get answers to where my cows went. Not only did you find them, and the thief, you went to a different world to bring them back."

I glanced at the check and smothered my surprise. Bills would get paid and I'd be able to get gas and groceries. Nice payday. As I was tucking the check into my pocket, my office door opened again. Ivan looked up in surprise and excused himself after another round of profuse thanks. Danny didn't move.

"What do you want?" I snapped.

"I believe I need your services," Wiley answered with a smirk.

"If you are hoping I can find your

balls, don't bother. I don't take on cases with impossible endings. I can't find what doesn't exist," I ground out. Danny coughed into his fist. "As you can see, I'm in a meeting at the moment. Make an appointment," I said, standing and pushing him out the door.

"I've left several messages already," Wiley whined.

"They'll get answered in the order received," I quipped and shut and locked the door before he could come back in. I looked at Danny. "Feel like wagging your tongue with someone that's been out of this world for some surf and turf?"

Michelle Lee is a Pacific Northwest native with a mind open to possibilities. Growing up, people often saw her with her face buried in a book and not much has changed. She's living her life dream of writing books that set her imagination free and explore the possibilities and mysteries she sees in the land all around her.

Find novel-length works by Michelle and additional *I S.P.I.* installments at:

www.BlueForgePress.com